Samantha's Silly-icious Sandwiches

With love to my father, James D'Alessandro. Thanks for introducing me to silly-icious sandwiches! With love to my mother, Jane D'Alessandro. Thanks for making all those school lunches!

– Tina Powell

The author also wishes to acknowledge Laura Petrie and Stephanie Howell. Thanks for bringing Samantha to life!

First Edition

Library and Archives Canada Cataloguing in Publication

Powell, Tina, 1962-

Samantha's silly-icious sandwiches / by Tina Powell ; illustrated by

Jenny Campbell.

ISBN 0-9737799-2-6

I. Campbell, Jenny II. Title.

PS8581.O8925S35 2006 jC813'.54 C2006-904882-7

Design by MAD marketing+design

Editing by Susan Petersiel Berg

Photography by Randy Powell

Printed in Canada by St. Joseph Print, Thorn

Samantha's Silly-icious Sandwiches

by Tina Powell

Illustrated by Jenny Campbell

Samantha opened her lunchbox and peeked inside. “Not another salami sandwich!” she cried. Samantha slammed the lid shut. “Why do I always get the same, old, boring sandwiches for lunch?”

Samantha looked around the classroom. Peter was sinking his teeth into a spicy sausage. Andrew was sipping some steaming soup. Even Ms. Sweetwater, the lunchroom supervisor, was savouring her spinach and strawberry salad. Everyone had a delicious lunch. Everyone except Samantha.

That night Samantha's mother opened Samantha's lunchbox and peeked inside.

"Not another salami sandwich!" she cried. She slammed the lid shut. "Samantha! You didn't eat any of your salami sandwich! And yesterday you didn't eat your Swiss cheese sandwich. Or your salmon sandwich the day before."

"Sheesh!" Samantha exclaimed. "Salami! Swiss cheese! Salmon! I'm sick of eating the same, old, boring sandwiches every day. All the other kids have lunches that are fun. All the other kids have lunches that are exciting."

Samantha's mother frowned. "I can be fun. I can be exciting. Watch this."

Samantha watched as her mother placed two slices of bread and a package of salami on the kitchen counter.

“Mom, that’s the same, old, boring sandwich you made for me today,” Samantha complained.

“Oh, no, it’s not,” Samantha’s mother smiled. “I’m going to put mustard on it.” Squirt! Squirt!

“Mustard? There’s nothing fun or exciting about mustard,” Samantha cried.

“How about ketchup?” suggested Samantha’s mother.

Samantha shook her head. “I bet I can make better sandwiches than that.” Suddenly, Samantha had an idea. “That’s it! I’ll make my own sandwiches for lunch!”

“You can’t be serious,” Samantha’s mother said suspiciously.

“Sandwiches are super-simple to make,” said Samantha. “I know I can do it!”

“Well, I could use a break from making your lunch every day,” Samantha’s mother admitted. “And if you make your own sandwiches, you might just eat them.”

Samantha squealed with delight. “It’s set! From now on, leave the sandwich-making to me!”

The next day Samantha brought a scrumptious spaghetti-and-sweet-pickle sandwich to school. She gave it a sniff! “Sure smells good,” she said. Samantha took a small bite. “Mmmmm, tastes even better.” Slurp! Scrump! Squish! Samantha munched on her sandwich.

Peter and Andrew sat down at Samantha's table. "Say! Is that spaghetti in your sandwich?" asked Peter.

"And sweet pickles?" asked Andrew.

"Yes," smiled Samantha, "and this sandwich tastes delicious!"

Andrew stood up and shouted, "Hey, everyone! Samantha has a spaghetti-and-sweet-pickle sandwich!"

"Shocking!" someone shouted.

"Silly!" snickered someone else.

Samantha licked the spaghetti sauce from her fingers. “Say what you want, my silly spaghetti-and-sweet-pickle sandwich tastes delicious. In fact, it’s silly-icious!”

The following day, the students all lined up to see Samantha's new silly-icious sandwich. She proudly showed it to them: a Salisbury-steak-and-scrambled-egg sandwich.

“What’s the red sauce smothered all over it?” asked Peter.

“Strawberry syrup,” giggled Samantha.

“And what are the crunchy bits?” asked Andrew.

“Sunflower seeds,” laughed Samantha.

“Would you like a taste?” she asked.

Peter took a tiny nibble. “Simply stupendous!” he shouted.

Andrew took a big bite. “Sensational!” he screamed.

Before Samantha could say, “Stop eating my silly-icious Salisbury-steak-and-scrambled-egg sandwich smothered in strawberry syrup and sunflower seeds,” her sandwich was gone.

Samantha sighed. “Tomorrow I will bring sandwiches to share.”

“This sweet-potato-and-succotash sandwich is wonderful!” cried Ms. Sweetwater.

“I love this stir-fried-shrimp-and-sushi submarine,” said Peter.

“Wait till you try the sardine-and-shish-kabob sandwich,” added Andrew.

Samantha’s silly-icious sandwiches were a smashing success! Everyone wanted them.

Always smart, Samantha had another idea. The next day she set up her own silly-icious sandwich stand.

"Get your silly-icious sandwiches here," Samantha shouted. "Only six dollars each!"

Every day the lineup at Samantha's Silly-icious Sandwich Stand got longer

and longer. And every day Samantha sold out of her silly-icious sandwiches.

Soon there were Samantha action figures, Silly-icious Sandwich video games, Samantha lunchboxes, and even a Silly-icious Sandwich song.

Samantha's mother was so proud. "I taught her everything she knows about sandwiches," she said to the reporters.

Surprisingly, Samantha was very sad. “This stinks,” she sniffed, holding back her tears. “Running a silly-icious sandwich empire is stressful. I have no time to see my friends. No time for singing in the choir. No time for soccer practice. And no time for Skip, my Shetland pony.”

Samantha sighed, “There must be some way I can stop all this sandwich silliness! If only things could go back to the way they were.”

Suddenly, Samantha smiled. “I know exactly what I need to do!”

The next day Samantha’s Silly-icious Sandwich Stand opened just like always, but Samantha’s customers were not satisfied.

“Is this some sort of a joke?” someone asked.

“I want my money back!” someone else cried. “Are you trying to make us sick?”

“Sick? Don’t be silly,” said Samantha. “From now on I’m only serving salami, Swiss cheese, or salmon sandwiches.”

“SHEESH!” everyone shouted. “There’s nothing fun or exciting about salami, Swiss cheese, or salmon! We’re not buying your silly-icious sandwiches anymore!”

Samantha smiled. “So long, Silly-icious Sandwich Stand,” she sang. “Hello, Peter, Andrew, soccer, singing, and Skip.”

The following day, Samantha opened her lunchbox and peeked inside. “I wonder what same, old, boring sandwich my mom made for me today. Is it salami? Or Swiss cheese? Or salmon?”

Samantha stared in shock and delight. “It’s a salami-Swiss-cheese-and-salmon sandwich with mustard and ketchup!” she shouted. “How can this be?”

Samantha ran to the classroom window and looked outside …

"Well," Samantha laughed. "I did teach her everything she knows about silly-icious sandwiches!"